THE MYSTERY AT

AT

Area 51

First Edition ©2011 Carole Marsh/Gallopade International/Peachtree City, GA
Current Edition ©2013
Ebook Edition ©2011
All rights reserved.
Manufactured in Peachtree City, GA

Carole Marsh Mysteries™ and its skull colophon are the property of Carole Marsh and
Gallopade International.

Published by Gallopade International/Carole Marsh Books. Printed in the United States
of America.

Editor: Janice Baker
Assistant Editor: Gabrielle Humphrey
Cover Design: John Hanson
Content Design: Randolyn Friedlander
Photo Credits: Istockphoto.com

Gallopade International is introducing SAT words that kids need to know in
each new book that we publish. The SAT words are bold in the story. Look for
each word in the special SAT glossary. Happy Learning!

Gallopade is proud to be a member and supporter of these educational organizations
and associations:

American Booksellers Association
American Library Association
International Reading Association
National Association for Gifted Children
The National School Supply and Equipment Association
The National Council for the Social Studies
Museum Store Association
Association of Partners for Public Lands
Association of Booksellers for Children
Association for the Study of African American Life and History
National Alliance of Black School Educators

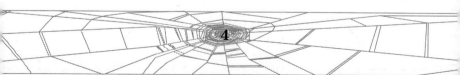

Once upon a time...

Hmm, kids keep asking me to write a mystery book. What shall I do?

Mimi

Write one about spiders!

You two really are characters, that's all I've got to say!

Yes you are! And, of course I choose you! But what should I write about?

National Parks!

SCARY PLACES!

Famous Places!

FUN PLACES!

Disney World!

New York City!

Dracula's Castle

GRAND CANYON

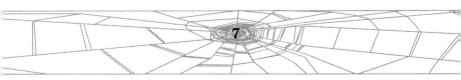

On the *Mystery Girl* airplane ...

I can FLY us anyWHeRe!

Or aboard
the *Mimi!*

Take me to the
Forbidden City!

Or by surfboard,
rickshaw,
motorbike,
camel ...

All great ideas!
I can put a lot of history,

MYSTERY,

legend, lore, and **laughs** in
the books! We can use other boys and girls
in the books. It will be educational and fun!

Good
stuff!

And so, Mimi, Papa, Christina, and Grant took off aboard the *Mystery Girl* and America's National Mystery Book Series—where the adventure is real and so are the characters! —was born.

START YOUR ADVENTURE TODAY!

READ THE BOOK!

GO ONLINE!

TRACK YOUR ADVENTURES!

APPLY TO BE A CHARACTER!

Yikes! That was close!

Rats!

1
A LITTLE TURBULENCE!

Christina unlocked her flower-patterned diary and set it in her lap. She ran her fingers over the embossed outer cover.

The last time Christina wrote in it was three years ago. She kept it in her glittery "keepsake shoebox" in the back of her closet—that is, until this trip.

"You've brought your diary, Christina," Mimi said over the roar of the airplane's engine. Mimi wore her blonde hair short. Her gem-studded glasses hung from her neck by a simple chain. She was "co-piloting" the *Mystery Girl* with her pilot husband, Papa. To her, he was a cowboy through and through. His tall rugged frame wouldn't be complete without a Stetson hat, jeans, and cowboy boots.

Christina and her younger brother, Grant, often traveled with their globe-trotting grandparents, Mimi and Papa, on vacation, while Mimi, a children's mystery writer, collected research for her books.

On this particular trip, Mimi planned to do research on Nevada mining ghost towns.

Their first stop—the Alamo, Nevada, landing strip of Papa's good friend, Mr. Colton Hayes. He went by "Buck," though, plain and simple. Buck and his wife, Nina, raised cattle on their 1,200-acre ranch.

"Yes, Mimi," Christina answered. "I brought this diary the first time we stayed at Buck's ranch three years ago."

"I remember that," Mimi said, smiling. "I recall that you got pretty good at drawing on that trip."

"Thanks, Mimi. I wish I could say the same about my spelling back then," Christina admitted. She tucked her long, brown hair behind her ears and looked over at Grant. He was fast asleep with his mouth gaping open. She turned to the first page of her diary. It read,

Propertey of Christina! Privite!

Christina fought the urge to correct her childish spelling. She continued to leaf through her diary and came to a page illustrated with desert flowers, their names obviously copied from an encyclopedia:

'*Hedgehog cactus*'–purple petals. '*Claret Cup cactus*'–red petals. '*Coulter's Lupine*'– purple and yellow.

Christina remembered the big lesson she learned three years ago: *Take only photographs. Leave only footprints.* She didn't have a camera, so she did the next best thing: she drew pictures–and lots of them!

Just then, a photo fell out of the diary and fluttered to the floor.

Christina hesitated before unbuckling her seatbelt, and then thought better of it. She flipped off her shoes, and using her toes, scooped up the photo.

Suddenly, the plane banked hard to the right. Her diary slid off her lap and disappeared under the seat in front of her.

Christina glanced back to check on her brother. The good news was that Grant was still buckled in. The bad news was he was upside down in his seat!

Is that even possible? she wondered.

Suddenly, Grant lifted his head, eyes still glued shut. "I want to put the spaceship together by myself!" he mumbled. Then, he plopped his head back down.

From the rumbling cockpit, Papa called out over his shoulder, "Minor turbulence! Nothing to worry about! Are you youngin's OK?"

"I'm fine!" Christina answered. "Grant is still sound asleep!"

Mimi looked over her shoulder and did a double-take. "He's really asleep like that?" she asked.

"Yep! He manages to be goofy even when he's asleep!" Christina joked. "Mimi, should we wake him up now?"

"Ten more minutes, OK?" Mimi said. "Otherwise, we'll have a little grouch on our hands."

Mimi leaned closer to Papa. Over the roar of the engine, Christina caught only a handful of words exchanged—near miss... strange object...mid-air...fifty-one...

Christina reached down to retrieve the photo from between her feet. She turned it over. In the picture, a younger Grant was standing in a giant tire swing hanging from an old oak tree. His bright blue eyes peered over the top of the tire. His signature curly-blonde hair framed a smiling face.

Megan and Drew, brother and sister, sat playing cards on a picnic blanket. They were about the same ages as Christina and Grant. Christina was standing under the tree, pointing at something in the sky. She looked puzzled.

Seeing herself in the old photo, Christina wondered, *What was I looking at in that blue November sky?*

Just then, Grant woke up from his dream with such a start that Christina jumped in her seat!

Grant's curly hair was matted down on one side. Christina couldn't help but laugh. "Grant, your hair!" she said and giggled.

Grant flipped right side up. He was annoyed at being laughed at, but was even more bothered that they let him sleep upside down.

"At least you didn't fall on your head, Grant," Christina teased. "You might have broken the floor!"

"Ha ha, you are such a genius!" Grant said.

"The correct term is child prodigy, little brother!" Christina said and laughed.

Christina looked out at the Mojave Desert through the plane's small window. Spiky cactus plants and Joshua trees dotted the landscape. There, on the **outskirts** of the desert, sprung an oasis of lush, green countryside.

"Mimi, look down!" Christina said. She popped the earphones out of her ears and stuffed her music player in her backpack.

"We must be close!" Mimi exclaimed.

"Finally!" Grant said.

"Well, crew, it looks like we're cleared for landing," Papa announced.

Christina's heart skipped a beat. She was eager to stand on solid ground. But she was nervous.

What if my old friends don't remember me? she thought.

"Look, I see Buck waving by the barn," Grant yelled. "Papa, I think he wants you to circle around," he warned.

"Grant's right, Papa! Look, there's a bull on the landing strip!" shouted Christina. "Buck needs to get him out of there!"

2
A CRIME AGAINST COWS

The *Mystery Girl* landed safely. Mimi hopped out onto the runway. Her red sneakers contrasted sharply with the black asphalt. The Nevada sun was beginning to set in the west.

Grant threw himself onto the ground. "Solid ground! You are my best friend in the whole wide world!" he cried.

"Grant! Here come Buck and Nina," Christina warned. She couldn't help but smile at her little brother's antics. He hopped up, ready to greet them.

A tall man with gray sideburns and sporting a white cowboy hat and leather boots approached the *Mystery Girl*. It was Buck, Papa's friend.

"Welcome to the Flyin' "R," folks! It's great to see ya'll again!" he roared.

Buck gave Papa a big bear hug. "Hello, good friend!" he said. "Sorry about that little inconvenience on the runway. Bulls and airplanes don't mix real well!"

His wife, Nina, a small, gray-haired woman, smiled warmly. Her hair was pulled back in a tidy bun. She wore a blue checkered apron over a t-shirt and jeans. Dust covered her tan cowboy boots.

"Buck and Nina, you remember Grant and Christina," Mimi said.

"My, you two have certainly grown!" Buck said. "The grandchildren are out getting supplies to make S'mores for the bonfire tonight."

"Megan and Drew begged their parents to let them come this week because they knew you two would be here!" Nina said.

Christina could finally exhale. *This vacation just might be something to write home about after all!*

Mimi and Nina walked ahead, arm-in-arm, chatting like no time had passed between visits.

Buck and Papa laughed heartily and slapped each other on the back as they unloaded the luggage from the plane.

At the ranch house, Mimi and the kids enjoyed tart homemade lemonade. Chunky ice cubes clinked in the tall glasses.

In the family room, a roaring fire burned brightly in a massive stone fireplace. Through a giant window bare of curtains, a pristine lake sparkled in the evening light. The setting sun cast brilliant hues of oranges and reds on the lake and the mountainous horizon beyond it.

"You all might want to freshen up a bit. We're having barbecue," Nina announced.

"Barbecue!" Grant shouted. He pumped his fist in the air. "I'm starving!"

"Oh, I hear Papa," Mimi said. "I'll be back in a minute."

The kids nodded. Nina led the way to their room. Her slippers slapped the floor as she walked. "Grant, quick, your shoes," Christina whispered, and pointed to Nina's retreating slippers. She gathered up their dusty sneakers.

Nina disappeared around a corner. Grant skated after her in his socks.

Christina heard Mimi and Papa talking in an adjacent room. "Mimi, what should I do with our shoes? Mimi?" She peeked in the room where she thought the voices were coming from but no one was there.

A long dining room table with enough chairs to seat an army sat in the middle of a massive dining room. A newspaper clipping lay on the middle of the table. Christina read it and gasped. She hurried from the room and ran smack into Grant!

Rubbing his head, Grant said, "Christina, where did you go?"

"Grant, you'll never believe what I just saw!" she exclaimed.

Grant's wide-eyed expression urged Christina to continue. "A newspaper article about cow abductions!"

"I've heard of cow patties, cowhide, and cows jumping over the moon, but I've never heard of cow and duck shins!" Grant said.

"Cow abductions, meaning cows being taken!" Christina exclaimed.

"Taken?" he asked. "Taken by who?"

"Not who! What!" she cried. "The newspaper article said it was aliens!" she exclaimed.

3
BREAKING BREAD, RANCH STYLE!

"Grant, what are you doing?" Christina asked.

"Checking for aliens, of course!" he said. "Under beds is the best place to hide! See, I found one of their socks!"

"I doubt there are any aliens in the house, Grant, aside from you, of course!" Christina teased. "We don't even know if that article is true!"

Christina walked over to a dresser lined with framed photos. She recognized Megan and Drew and their parents, and, of course, Buck and Nina.

One photo stood out, though. It was of a man with long gray hair. He wore typical ranch-hand clothes, but sported a gem-stoned bolo tie. And his face, though weathered and worn, gave no clue to his age.

Grant was leafing through a book.

"What's that?" Christina asked, joining him on the floor.

"I found a pile of UFO books on that bookshelf," Grant said. A bug-eyed alien jumped off the page. It had a protruding **abdomen**, thin legs, and long, bony fingers.

"Ooh, it looks too real!" she exclaimed and jumped up.

Grant tossed the book on the bedside table. "I call this bed!" he announced, and proceeded to jump up and down on it. The pillow sprang off onto the floor and the covers tangled into a lumpy mess.

"Fine with me! I call the shower, then!" Christina grabbed her overnight bag and practically slid in her socks to the bathroom. She felt refreshed after taking a shower and putting on clean clothes.

In the hallway she met a soap-scrubbed and freshly clothed Grant. "How did you...?" Christina began.

"You didn't hear Nina tell me about the other bathroom! Ha! That means I win—the bed and the first shower!" Grant teased his big sister.

"You!" Christina yelled. She chased Grant down the hall and into the family room.

"Christina, Grant!" Megan and Drew shouted in unison. They ran over to greet them. Megan was tall, like Christina. She wore her dark hair pulled back in a ponytail. Drew's hair was red and curly, more like his dad's in the photo. He had an athletic build and lots of freckles.

Megan continued shyly, "Nina says you're probably starving after your long trip. We brought barbecue!" Megan took Christina's hand and led her to the spacious kitchen. The boys were already piling food onto their plates when the girls arrived.

On the kitchen island sat mounds of tangy chicken wings, spare ribs, and beef brisket, along with heaps of baked beans, potato salad, corn on the cob, and giant slices of cornbread.

"It's a meal fit for a cowboy!" shouted Grant, crunching his teeth into a crisp ear of corn.

"Nina," said Mimi, "this is delicious!"

"It certainly hit the spot," agreed Papa, patting his stomach. He wiped the last traces of sauce from his mouth.

"Unfortunately, I can't take credit for any of this. Ol' Zeb picked this up while he was out getting S'more supplies with Megan and Drew," Nina admitted.

"We'll have dessert later," Buck announced. "In the meantime, we old folks will be in the sitting room if you need us."

"Ol' Zeb is about finished with the bonfire," Nina told the kids. "He'll let you know when it's ready."

4
DRAWING STRAWS!

BANG! BANG!

The kids instinctively ducked. They scurried to the kitchen window and peered out. Nothing!

"It's too dark!" Grant exclaimed.

BANG!

"There it is again!" Megan shouted. "Drew, get the flashlights!"

Drew retrieved four flashlights from the hall closet. The kids grabbed their shoes and jackets before heading outside.

They inched along in the dark. "I guess this means no S'mores tonight, huh?" Grant asked, disappointed.

"I have the stuff to make them, just in case," Megan whispered, patting her backpack.

BANG! They dropped to the ground at once.

Footsteps! A bright light shone down on them. "What are you doing out here?" a deep voice boomed. "Megan, Drew! You were supposed to wait until I came for you and your friends!"

The kids stood up and dusted themselves off.

"Sorry, Ol' Zeb. We heard loud noises," Megan explained.

Ol' Zeb swung the load he was carrying over his shoulders onto the ground. THUMP! Dust rose, then settled. The kids pointed their flashlights at the ground. Christina screamed.

Snakes! And one of them was still alive! The doomed creature made one last attempt at a rattle, then fell limp. Drew looked closely at the pile of reptiles. "Wow! They've been shot!" he shouted.

"These here are Great Basin rattlesnakes. One bite and you're a goner!" Ol' Zeb said.

"How can you tell they're venomous?" Grant asked, completely entranced.

"The triangular shape of the face," Zeb explained. "The rattle. The fat body. And see these distinctive black markings? Well, don't forget 'em! And remember," he paused for dramatic effect, "he won't always rattle before he strikes!"

"Oooooooh!" the kids said.

"You shot these?" asked Drew, impressed.

"Yes, siree! I got 'em before they got you!" Ol' Zeb's eyes shone brightly in the moonlight.

Christina recognized Ol' Zeb from the photo in their room. Despite her jacket, Christina felt goose bumps rise up on her arms.

He cackled, picked up the dead snakes, and swung them over his shoulder. "I reckon that bonfire is perfect for making S'mores now."

"Who *was* that?" Christina asked Megan after Ol' Zeb trudged away.

"That's 'Ol Zeb. When he's not helping out around the ranch, he spends his time scanning the skies for alien radio transmissions," Megan said.

"Really?" asked Grant.

"Yeah! He's got all these antennas and stuff sticking out of his trailer," Drew explained.

"That's weird!" Christina said.

"Not for around here," Drew said. "Area 51 attracts those kind of people. You'll see!"

What's Area 51, and why are UFO fanatics attracted to it? Christina wondered.

Megan interrupted her thoughts. "Now, let's do some S'moring!" Megan suggested.

"S'moring, huh? Did you make that up?" Christina asked and giggled.

Logs were already in place around the roaring fire. Megan laid out the S'more ingredients on separate plates: graham crackers, chocolate, and marshmallows.

The kids scanned the ground for long marshmallow-roasting sticks, but came up empty-handed.

"Let's draw straws!" Grant suggested, grabbing a pile of small twigs. "Whoever picks the shortest twig loses and has to look for marshmallow sticks."

Christina picked first. When she saw that Grant's was shorter, she put hers behind her back and broke off a piece.

"OK, everyone, show me your twigs," Grant said excitedly. "Sorry, Christina, you lose."

"Fine, I'll go, but on one condition," Christina said. "I get to make mine first!"

Everyone agreed. Christina headed for the ranch house. She scoured the ground for fallen branches. Nothing! Then she spied the outline of an enormous tree about the length of a football field away.

"OK, here goes!" she said to herself, gathering courage. She took off running through the pitch-black pasture with only her flashlight to guide her. *Drawing straws! What a silly game,* she thought. *We could have gone together to look for sticks!*

As she approached the tree, she saw the familiar tire swing from the photo! She scanned the ground. Suddenly, she heard the snap of ground cover behind her!

"Who's there?!" Christina yelled and swung around. Her bright yellow flashlight flew out of her hand and into the darkness.

"OWWW!" someone cried. It was Grant!

"Christina, I found you!" he shouted, relieved to have found his sister but mad that she was such a good shot. "Here's your weapon back!" He rubbed his elbow where the flying flashlight had made contact.

"Sorry about that!" Christina said. "Hey, what are you doing out here? *I'm* supposed to find the sticks!"

"That's why I came to get you," Grant began, still out of breath from running. "Hey, a tire swing!"

"Focus, Grant!" Christina warned.

"Oh, yeah. Ol' Zeb found sticks for us!" Grant explained. "He didn't want us running around in the dark."

"Fine by me!" Christina said. She turned on her heels to head back. "Grant, come on. Grant! We can do the tire swing some other time." She reached out to tug on his jacket. "Let's..."

Grant was staring at something hovering above the tree. A disc-shaped object, about the size of the outer canopy of the oak tree, floated just above them. Its whirling lights and buzzing noises practically hypnotized her brother.

"Grant, it's a UFO!" Christina yelped. "Let's get out of here!" Her plea must have broken the spell because Grant slowly stepped backwards from the tree. He suddenly whirled around and broke out in a full sprint. Christina raced behind him.

"The aliens are coming! The aliens are coming!" Grant shouted.

Christina caught up to her brother and grabbed his jacket to stop him.

"What's wrong? Why did we stop?" Grant asked, glancing back at the tree. The UFO was gone!

Christina wanted to tell him that she remembered what she was pointing at in the photo, but instead she said, "Let's do the secret handshake, Grant. Now!"

"What for?" Grant asked. Then, he understood: if they told anyone what they had just seen, their vacation would surely be over!

What Christina and Grant didn't notice was Ol' Zeb hiding in a grove of trees not fifty feet from them. His leathery face showed no expression at all. And then he was gone!

5
STICKY STUFF!

Christina and Grant returned, out of breath. "Grant found you!" Megan said, relieved.

The glow of the crackling fire danced on the nearby trees. An occasional airborne spark floated up and away with the wind.

Megan secured her unruly hair back in a ponytail. "Here, you choose first, Christina, just like we agreed." Megan showed her the sticks lying in a neat row on the ground.

"Thanks!" Christina said. She picked one up, grabbed a marshmallow, and started roasting it over the fire. The others did the same.

Grant and Drew weren't having much luck. They either burned their marshmallows to a crisp or ended up with a gooey mess. Either way, they had fun flicking the rejects into the fire and starting over.

Christina and Megan watched eagerly as their toasted marshmallows melted the sweet chocolate sandwiched between the graham crackers. "Mmm, mmm, good!" they mumbled through sticky bites. Marshmallow and cracker bits clung to their teeth.

The girls kept the supply of toasted marshmallows flowing to their brothers. The boys insisted on doing the rest themselves, so more crackers ended up in the dirt than in their stomachs.

Suddenly, Grant leaped to his feet and ran around the group waving a burning marshmallow on the end of a stick. "Look, a UFO—*an unidentified flaming object*!" he shouted.

Christina shot Grant a stern look to remind him of their pact. Luckily, Megan was too busy pulling a melted marshmallow out of Drew's hair to notice.

"Hey," said Drew, "I've got an alien joke."

"Tell me!" Grant cried.

"What do you call an alien spaceship that drips water?" Drew asked.

Grant shrugged. "I don't know—what?"

"A crying saucer!" Drew replied.

Grant roared with laughter while the girls giggled. Megan turned her attention back to their snack. "We're out of graham crackers!" she announced.

"There's one pack left!" Christina said. She handed it to Megan and tossed the empty box into the flames.

A piece of paper fluttered to the ground at her feet. It was the store receipt for the S'more supplies. Without balling it up first, Christina tried to toss it into the fire. It blew back to her.

She leaned down to pick it up. On the back of the receipt was a message written in hurried scrawl:

SBJ06201833

The stone points the way to the silent mouth!

A clue? Out here in the middle of nowhere? As if nearly colliding with something mid-air, news of abducted cattle, seeing dead snakes, and witnessing a UFO weren't enough for one day! Christina thought.

She slipped the note into her jacket pocket. A mystery was definitely unfolding!

6
MIND YOUR MANNERS!

The RV that Mimi and Papa rented for their sightseeing tour sat parked in front of the ranch house. Grant and Drew crawled around inside it, inspecting the cool gadgets and peeking inside cabinets.

"Drew, check this out!" Grant yelled. He turned a lever on the floor and pulled up on the handle. A hidden table popped up and unfolded to full-size.

"Whoa!" Drew said, thoroughly impressed. "Look at this!" He opened a small door under one of the cushioned benches and crawled inside. Grant tried the other door and disappeared, too. Giggles echoed from inside the cubbyholes.

The bright Nevada sun was already high in the sky. Papa and Buck were busy attaching a trailer to the back of the RV.

"Christina, Mimi tells me you know how to drive a four-wheeler," said Nina. Nina and Mimi were in the kitchen boxing up supplies to take on the trip.

"Yes, ma'am! Grant can, too!" Christina answered.

"That'll come in handy where you're going. Some of the old mining towns around here aren't completely accessible by car," Nina said.

"Nina, can we load them up now?" asked Megan hopefully.

Nina nodded. "Come on, Christina!" Megan squealed. The girls raced to the barn. It took them three trips to drive all six four-wheelers onto the trailer.

"Nice work, girls!" Papa said, as he fastened the last of the vehicles down with safety straps. Buck slammed the trailer tailgate shut and announced, "You're good to go!"

"Remember, Drew and Megan, mind your manners!" Nina warned gently.

"We will, Nina!" they answered and bounded into the RV. The kids waved good-bye one last time through the back window of the RV as it pulled away down the long, winding dirt road towards the highway.

"Buckle up!" Papa bellowed. "First stop, the mining ghost town of Tybo, Nevada!" Papa headed north towards Highway 93, electing to take the route that ran parallel to the highway.

7
A RIBBON IN THE DESERT

Richardville Road, the scenic route that hugs Highway 93, was dotted with ranches, alfalfa fields, and tall cottonwoods.

"Wow! It's like an oasis!" Grant exclaimed.

"That's because we're smack dab in the middle of Pahranagat Valley!" Papa explained.

"This part of the valley is the most fertile," Megan added. "It's not that big—only a mile wide and about forty miles long."

"And from the air," Papa said, "it looks like a...Mimi, how did you describe it?"

"Like a green ribbon lost in the Nevada desert!" Mimi answered poetically. Papa smiled. "That's my girl!" he said.

Drew added, "The ranches around here grow a lot of alfalfa."

"Falafel? I thought falafel were fried chickpea balls. You can grow falafel balls right in the ground?" Grant asked.

"Alfalfa, not falafel," said Christina and giggled. "But why do they grow so much of it here?"

"Cattle love it!" Megan said. "It's one of the hays that grows really well here—something to do with hot days and cool nights. It grows really fast, too, so they harvest it several times a year."

"Hey!" Grant said. "That's a lot of alfalfa *hay*!" Grant was secretly proud of his *hey-hay* **homonym** usage. "The cows around here must be pretty happy!"

Megan and Drew looked at each other. "I wish the same could be said about *our* cattle," Drew said quietly.

"Is something wrong?" Christina asked, remembering the newspaper clipping about the cattle abductions.

Megan and Drew nodded. "Someone or *something* has been stealing the cattle from Buck and Nina's ranch," Drew explained.

"Not only from theirs, but from other ranches, too! Some people are saying that aliens are responsible," Megan said.

"What do you think?" Christina asked.

"Well, we haven't seen any spaceships or aliens, but...this is going to sound weird. We have found crop circles in our field," Megan said.

"Crop circles?" Grant asked.

"Crop circles are supposedly patterns left behind by alien spacecraft," Christina said. "The crops are found pressed down, not torn up, like something heavy pushed down on them."

"I personally think it's a hoax, but the newspapers seem really sure aliens are involved," Megan said. Christina and Grant exchanged glances.

"What? You don't believe any of that stuff, do you?" Megan continued. "No one's been able to prove that aliens even exist."

"Megan, Grant and I saw something last night near that old oak tree," Christina whispered. She felt bad about breaking her pact with Grant and looked at him.

"It's OK," Grant said sheepishly. "I kinda mentioned it to Drew already."

"What did you see?" pressed Megan.

Christina related the events of the night before. "It was like Grant was hypnotized by the whirling lights!" she said.

Megan and Drew looked shocked. "Maybe the aliens in that spaceship came to steal more cattle!" Drew said.

"The UFO we saw was too small for that," Christina said.

"No, they probably have huge ones for sucking up the cattle," Grant said.

"Wow, you think?" Drew said, impressed with Grant's knowledge of alien spacecraft.

"I thought we were just going to visit some old mining towns. Now, we're in the middle of some cow-napping alien mystery! Why can't we have a normal trip for once?" Christina groaned.

8
TOP SECRET!

Papa was focused on the road ahead of him. The engine rumbled and backfired. Then, it hummed again. Everyone breathed a collective sigh of relief.

Papa veered off the scenic route and merged onto Highway 93. He stopped for gas in Ash Springs, "the only town with a gas station for miles," according to one customer just leaving the gas station.

Papa announced, "Hang on, kids! We're heading west onto the last stretch of highway before the ghost mining town of Tybo!"

"Cool!" Grant shouted. "Maybe we'll get to meet a real ghost!"

"A ghost town doesn't always have ghosts, Grant. It just means no one lives there anymore," lectured Christina.

Papa said, "Tybo wasn't a peaceful settlement. Different cultures meant different ways of doing things. This led to many saloon brawls and, unfortunately, to many unmarked graves!"

"Then there may be ghosts after all!" Grant said hopefully.

"We just passed through Rachel!" Megan announced.

"Is Rachel a ghost?" Grant asked.

"What? No!" Megan said and laughed. "It's a town."

"Rachel's a pretty cool town, if you're into UFOs and amazing burgers," Drew added.

"Yummy! Burgers!" Grant exclaimed. "Mimi, can we go to Rachel?"

"That's next on the itinerary," Mimi replied. "We'll go to Tybo first, while it's still early."

"OK," Grant said. Then he turned to Drew and asked, "Is Rachel a ghost town, too, because it doesn't sound very ghostly."

"It's not a ghost town," Drew explained. "It's a tourist town next to Area 51."

"What's Area 51, anyway?" Grant asked.

"It's the code name for a secret aircraft and weapons testing facility surrounding Groom Lake. It's kinda top secret," Drew said.

"You mean the 'I can tell you, but I'll have to kill you' kind of top secret?" asked Grant with a mischievous grin.

"Yeah, that kind," Drew answered, nodding.

Grant expected Drew to say, "Oh, just kidding." Only an uncomfortable silence followed. Grant gulped loudly.

"Speaking of codes," Christina said, "I found this last night."

"It's just the S'more receipt," Megan said, unimpressed.

"No, on the back," Christina said. She turned it over and read the clue. "SBJ06201833. The stone points the way to the silent mouth!"

"Where did you find this?" Megan asked.

"By the bonfire," Christina replied. "I almost tossed it in the fire last night by accident."

"What do you think it means?" Grant asked Christina. He tried to sound like none of this was scaring him, but his trembling voice gave him away.

"I have no idea!" Christina exclaimed.

9

GHOST TOWNS AND GRAVEYARDS

Papa pulled off the highway and drove down miles of unmarked dirt roads until he arrived in Tybo, a old Shoshone Indian word for "white man's district."

Mimi chose a picnic site that overlooked the picturesque Tybo canyon. "At one time," Mimi began, "Tybo was a bustling silver mining community."

Now, it was quiet. Wind whistled through old mining structures and small abandoned buildings. Two brick charcoal kilns rose up like giant ant hills.

"In its heyday in the late 1800s," Mimi explained, "Tybo had 1,000 residents, plus a post office and a newspaper. See that gutted brick building? It used to be a schoolhouse.

Even though the adults didn't always get along, the children all went to the same school.

"Unfortunately, when mining production dropped, so did the town's population," she continued. "Over the years, new mining companies came to Tybo to seek their fortune. Tybo always managed to produce more silver, and the population would rise, but never like at its peak," Mimi explained.

"Now, it's a ghost town, right?" Grant asked.

Mimi nodded.

"Can we go exploring?" Christina asked.

"Absolutely!" Mimi said. "You might even find some hidden gold! I read that the Tybo residents didn't trust the banks, so they buried their gold coins instead!"

The kids raced off when they heard they might find buried gold. Mimi chuckled and turned back to her research notebook.

The terrain wasn't easy to navigate on the four-wheelers. It was rocky, and everywhere you looked brush sprouted from the desert floor in clumps.

"The schoolhouse!" Grant shouted. "Looks like school's out—permanently!"

"What's that on the hill?" Christina asked.

"It looks like a cemetery," said Megan.

"Whoa!" Grant exclaimed. "Let's go see those unmarked graves that Papa was talking about!" They raced up the hill.

The graveyard was in disarray. Gravestones jutted out of the ground every which way. Most appeared forgotten or had no headstone at all.

Christina and Megan crawled over vegetation to get a better look at a broken headstone leaning against a granite base. The letters were still legible after more than 100 years!

"This lady died in 1882 at only 59!" Megan, said, fingering the faint etching on the headstone. "She was from Massachusetts and I'll bet she followed her husband here for work."

"Look at this one!" Christina shouted. She unfolded the receipt in her pocket. "You're not going to believe this! I think the clue is this headstone! See? The letters are the initials of his name, SBJ, and the numbers refer to his birth date, June 20, 1833!"

"You're right!" Grant agreed. He read the rest of the clue. "The stone points the way to the silent mouth!"

"The gravestone points that way, Grant, towards the hillside," Christina said.

"Well, what are we waiting for?!" Grant shouted.

10

CAVE COWBOYS

Climbing the craggy hillside was a challenge. The kids grunted and groaned as drops of sweat beaded on their foreheads.

"I see something up ahead," Christina yelled.

The kids dusted off their clothes and studied the entrance to what appeared to be a cave. Thick brush blocked the entrance.

They pulled the brush aside and peered inside. "It's an abandoned mine shaft!" Drew declared.

"Did anyone bring a flashlight?" Grant asked.

"You're not seriously thinking of going inside, are you? Why do you think they're called *abandoned* mine shafts?" Megan asked.

"Someone left this clue for us," Christina reasoned.

"But, what if that 'someone' is trying to get us hurt?" Megan replied.

"We'll be careful, I promise!" Christina said. "If it looks too dangerous, we'll crawl out." Megan cringed at the thought of "crawling out" of anything.

"All of the four-wheelers have flashlights. I'll go run and get them," Drew offered.

"I'll go with you," said Megan.

Christina watched them disappear down the hill. "It'll take at least fifteen minutes for them to come back, Grant. Grant?" Christina repeated. Grant was gone!

Christina crawled gingerly into the mine shaft after her brother. "Grant," she whispered. Nothing! She moved further into the tunnel.

It's so dark! Any second now I'll slide down some slippery, cold hole and get stuck, Christina feared.

"Ohhhh!" Christina cried. Her hand brushed against something hairy!

"Christina, it's just me, Grant," he whispered. "Stop grabbing my hair! There are people down there! Come on!"

"I'm coming!" Christina whispered. She couldn't see her brother, but she could hear him shuffling ahead of her.

The tunnel turned and dove deeper. A chill hung in the air. Just then, a man's voice whispered into Christina's ear, "Go back! Go back!" Christina froze. Something tugged at her jacket. She reached behind her in the darkness. No one was there!

Christina pulled on Grant's shirt and squealed, "Did you hear that?"

"I didn't say anything," he answered, misunderstanding her question.

The narrow tunnel gradually lit up as they turned the corner. An exit! Christina covered her mouth when she looked down. It wasn't an exit at all! *It must be one hundred feet down from here! No wonder it was abandoned!* she thought.

A huge underground cave opened up in front of them. A rusty track ran the length of the cavern below. It splintered off into more tunnels.

From their perch, Christina and Grant saw four men dressed in cowboy hats and boots. Dangling kerosene lanterns cast eerie shadows on the cave walls. The men pointed to maps and photographs lying on a slab of rock. The words 'cattle,' 'ranches,' and 'UFOs' floated up to them.

Something fluttered above Christina's head. She ducked and swatted it away. It was fuzzy! She ducked again, but it was too late! Something was tangled in her hair, flapping and whacking her scalp.

"Christina," Grant whispered frantically, "it's a bat!"

"AHHHHHHHHHH!" Christina screamed and stood up, banging her head on the tunnel roof. The bat struggled one last time and finally freed itself from her hair. It darted deeper into the cave.

"Hey, who's up there?" a man shouted, spying two pair of wide eyes peering at him from the children's hiding place. But that was the last thing the men saw before being engulfed by a whirling, diving colony of bats.

Grant and Christina scrambled out so fast they nearly bowled over Megan and Drew waiting at the entrance.

"Here are the flashlights," Megan said.

"Forget the flashlights! Run!" Grant shouted.

The kids frantically navigated the four-wheelers over bumps and dips. Christina waved the others to follow her to a worn path. She stopped when the path met the parking lot.

"The RV...is just...on the other side...of those trees," Christina said, out of breath.

"Look, a truck!" Grant shouted. "Maybe it belongs to those guys in the mine!" A "My Other Truck Is a Pair of Boots!" bumper sticker adorned the back bumper of the dusty black truck jacked up on enormous tires.

"It must belong to them! No one else is out here," Christina said.

"Someone's coming!" Grant whispered. The kids peeled out in a hurry and arrived back at the RV safely, hearts still beating wildly from their adventure.

"Perfect timing!" roared Papa. "Round up those vehicles and get them onto the trailer. We gotta get a move on! Next stop, Rachel, Nevada!"

Once inside the RV, the kids felt safe and moved to the back to relax. The weathered Tybo welcome sign rattled gently in the wind. To Christina, it seemed to be waving goodbye.

ROOOOAAAARRRRR! The kids peered out the window to see the huge black truck pass by the RV. The driver, with his tan cowboy hat pulled down low on his forehead, glared at the kids as he sped by.

11
A PUZZLE IN A POCKET

"That was close!" Grant exclaimed and sunk deep in his seat.

"What do you think those guys were doing down in the mine?" Megan asked.

"Probably looking for some hidden gold!" Drew guessed.

Megan noticed that Christina was lost in thought. "Is something wrong, Christina?" she asked.

"Back in the tunnel, I think a ghost whispered to me!" Christina replied. "He said, 'Go back! Go back!'"

"I bet it was a ghost afraid we'd find his buried gold!" Grant joked.

"This is no joke! I really heard it! He tugged on my jacket!" Christina said.

"Sometimes voices travel, Christina," Megan suggested.

Remembering the eerie voice, Christina stuffed her hands into her jacket pockets as a chill ran down her spine.

"Voices may travel, but envelopes sure can't!" Christina exclaimed, pulling something from her pocket. "I knew I felt a tug on my jacket!" In her hand was a faded envelope sealed shut with the letters SBJ stamped in wax!

"Aren't those the same initials from the clue—the ones on the headstone?" Megan asked in disbelief. Christina nodded.

"Are you going to open it or are we going to stare at it all day?" Grant asked, eager to see what was inside.

"You do it!" Christina said and shoved it into Grant's hand. "I've had enough surprises for one day!"

Grant peeled the wax seal back and opened the envelope. "It's another clue!" he announced.

HC6ISR375
Things are not always
as they appear!

"This clue makes zero sense to me," Christina said.

"It might be a phone number; the letters could stand for numbers, right?" Drew suggested.

"It doesn't look long enough to be a phone number," Grant noted. "What about a license plate number?"

"It looks more like an address to me," Megan said. "HC stands for Highway Contract. With an HC address, you *do* get mail, but it won't come in a regular mail truck."

"Oh, I know! It comes in a spaceship, right?" Grant joked.

"Yep," Drew answered matter-of-factly.

"Huh, really?" Grant asked.

"Nah," Drew said, "JK—that's text lingo for 'just kidding.'"

"Uh, I know what it stands for!" Grant said, sounding irritated.

Christina knew he didn't really know that and rolled her eyes. "Hey, Drew, you just gave me an idea." Christina pulled out her cell phone. She pulled up her Internet application and searched for the code HC61SR375. "Nothing!" she said.

"Try separating 'HC' from 61," Megan suggested.

"Nope, still no matches," Christina said.

"Try separating all the letters from the numbers," Grant said.

Christina entered HC 61 SR 375. "Look at this!" she said. "The Little A'Le'Inn in Rachel, Nevada! Wait! *Rachel*, Nevada?" Christina repeated, stunned. "That's where Papa said we're headed!"

"Little Alien?" Grant exclaimed. "What kind of place are we going to, anyway? This trip is getting more and more out of this world!"

12

BONY FINGERS!

As the RV rumbled down the desolate highway, Mimi drifted off to sleep. Papa fiddled with the radio, then gave up when all he got was static.

The kids began to feel antsy. They fanned themselves with the paper plates Christina pulled from the cabinet.

"I can't take it anymore!" Grant shouted and stood up. "My sweat is gluing my collar to my neck! Christina, can't you open that window any faster? I feel like I'm stuck in a tin can on wheels!"

"I'm trying, Grant," Christina answered, trying not to laugh at his analogy. "It's not budging!"

"That's one of those picture windows. They don't open," Drew pointed out.

"OK, smarty pants," Megan said. "Then which of these windows does open?" Sweat beaded on her upper lip.

"How should I know?" he shot back.

"Well, you spent enough time playing in here before we left!" Megan said accusingly.

"OK, OK! I'll just ask Mimi," Christina said, trying to keep the peace.

"Mimi," Christina whispered. She gently tapped her on the shoulder. "I'm sorry to wake you, but it's getting pretty hot back here."

"Oh, dear," Mimi said, still half-asleep, "Papa, the air's not working in the back. Papa?" Mimi repeated.

Papa was listening to one of his audio books. Mimi gently pulled the earphone bud from his right ear.

"Papa, the air doesn't work in the back. The kids are burning up," Mimi said. Suddenly, the engine rumbled and coughed again.

"Looks like we might be having some engine trouble too," Papa said. Smoke billowed from the engine. "But not to worry!" he exclaimed. "We have arrived!"

The old RV squeaked to a halt. Papa turned around in his seat and announced, "Little A'Le'Inn! Rachel, Nevada! Home to UFOs and alien burgers!"

"Good, 'cause I'm starving!" Grant squealed. "I sure hope alien meat tastes as good as regular hamburger meat."

"Ooh, Grant! That's gross!" Christina said.

Grant swung the door open and hopped out. The others scrambled out behind him. Megan reached to close the door behind her, but the door banged shut by itself!

A small, pale-skinned man wearing dark sunglasses stood inches from Grant's nose! His bony fingers held the RV door shut.

"Watch it, earthlings!" he squeaked. "You dented my ship!" He pointed at Grant, who had unknowingly banged the RV door into the side of the car next to it. Next, he eyed the smoke snaking out of the RV's hood and leaned over to sniff it. "Hmmm," he murmured, and slid into his beat-up, rusty sedan. As he caressed the dented door through the open window, he did a countdown, "5, 4, 3, 2, 1, BLAST OFF!" The little man backed up and screeched out of the parking lot. The kids watched him leave, their mouths open in amazement.

"You weren't kidding when you said Area 51 attracts strange characters!" Christina mumbled to her friends.

The kids noticed a giant sign out front. Two boulders supported its legs. The top half of the sign advertised a restaurant, a bar, and a motel. The bottom half read:

EARTHLINGS WELCOME
LITTLE
A'LE'INN

Parked in the shadow of the sign was a rusty, white tow truck. Weeds grew in its shade. Floating from a chain attached to the back of the truck was a shiny, round UFO-like object gleaming in the sun.

"I get the gray rock!" Grant shouted.

"I call the white one!" Drew announced. They raced to the sign and climbed onto the boulders. The girls walked over to admire the metal UFO.

"Over here, kids! Say 'alien'!" Mimi shouted, and snapped a picture of the group. She texted Nina to tell her a photo was on its way.

13
A, B, C, D, AND FRIES!

Papa held open the blue door of the Little A'Le'Inn restaurant for Mimi and the children. Cool air filtered out of the restaurant, carrying with it the mouth-watering smell of grilled burgers and french fries.

A family of seven filed out. They were dressed like aliens, with green-painted faces, bouncing antennae, and skin-tight bodysuits. Their fluorescent-green scuba fins slapped the pavement. In the sunlight, the costumes shimmered an out-of-this-world purple and green.

Last to exit was Alien Mom pushing a stroller. The kids leaned down, curious to see if Baby Alien matched the others. "Nope, no green paint," noted Grant. "But he does have a really cool pacifier!"

Baby Alien yanked the blinking blue, red, and green spaceship pacifier out of his mouth and babbled baby sounds. "He recommends the A, B, C, D, and fries!" Alien Mom said. The green paint on her face crinkled as she smiled.

"A, B, C, D?" asked Christina.

"Alien Burger with Cheese and a Drink, of course!" She slid open the side door of the waiting minivan and strapped her baby into his seat. The driver revved the engine. The door automatically slid shut, and they were off! The words "Aliens Rock!" were scrawled in the dust on the back window of the minivan.

"That one takes the cake!" Drew said.

"I kinda thought Bony Fingers back there was pretty cool," said Grant.

"Yeah, creepy, but cool," Drew agreed. Walking into the Little A'Le'Inn was like entering another world. Eerie music filled the air. Area 51 posters and framed newspaper articles on alien sightings covered the walls. Shelves near the cash register displayed souvenirs for sale while shiny green alien blow-up toys floated above them.

They sat down at a school-cafeteria-style table and quickly ordered Baby Alien's recommended meal. "Yep, this was the best choice," Grant mumbled between greasy bites. Drew nodded, ketchup dripping from his chin.

While Mimi and Papa chatted with the friendly owners of the Little A'Le'Inn, the kids explored the restaurant.

Christina and Megan perused the CD collection while the boys examined the toys for sale.

"I bet you want one of those cool spaceship pacifiers, too!" Grant said to a realistic-looking alien propped up in a highchair.

After a while, Mimi joined the children at the rotating postcard stand. "I'm going to visit the ladies room," she said. "Papa went to check on the RV. I'll be back in a flash." She disappeared into the restroom.

"Look, Grant, an alien with antlers!" Drew snorted, pointing to a holiday postcard.

"A few years back, I had a close encounter!" began a tourist with an "I See Aliens" button pinned to his vest jacket.

The kids inched closer to the table to eavesdrop.

The blonde, petite woman sitting across from the man looked at him like he was suffering from some sort of **ailment**. She quickly excused herself and moved to another table.

Seeing that he still had an audience, the man picked up where he left off.

"I was on my way here to this very locale to meet my buddy," he began. "Back then, it was the Rachel Bar and Grill. Little A'Le'Inn is more fitting, if you ask me!" he added.

"Anyways, I was in the middle of the Nevada desert, when the headlights on my truck started flickering on and off! The radio dial did this crazy dance. Then, the radio went dead! My truck started spinning out of control!"

The man's eyes grew wide. "When it stopped, a bright light flooded in. My truck started to rise off the ground! I tried to get out, but the door wouldn't budge! There was no way I was getting sucked up into that spaceship, so I climbed out the back window and made a jump for it. It had to have been twenty feet!

"I broke my arm when I landed," he continued. "See? Here's the scar!" A red, angry scar ran the length of his forearm.

The kids gasped. "Aww," the man said, "a broken arm ain't nothing compared to some alien sucking the brains right out of my head! Anyways, just then, the UFO and my truck disappeared into thin air!"

"Did you ever find it—your truck, I mean?" Grant asked.

"You betcha, I did!" he said. "A week later, out of nowhere, it appeared in the middle of the highway. And there were *witnesses*! Thing is, every wire in that truck was stripped, even from the hard-to-get-to places!"

Grant and Christina involuntarily covered their mouths with their hands: Grant out of fear, Christina to hide a giggle.

14
DID YOU HEAR THAT?

BOOM! Christina and Grant moved their hands from their mouth to their ears in one swift motion and ducked. The boom was so loud the floor shook!

They stood up, mouths open in utter disbelief. No one seemed at all surprised by what just happened! In fact, it was business as usual.

One employee straightened the knickknacks on the shelves and righted the pictures on the wall. Another grabbed a broom and swept up some broken glass. It was as if no one felt the boom except them!

"Mimi! Did you hear that?" Grant asked when he saw Mimi exit the restroom. "It was so loud it knocked pictures off the wall!"

"*That* was a sonic boom, Grant," Mimi said. "Rachel is the sonic boom capital of the world!"

"That was a sonic boom?" he asked. "Doesn't that happen when jets fly at supersonic speeds?"

"Yes," Mimi replied. "When a jet moves faster than the speed of sound, it creates a lot of pressure. It's the change in pressure that creates that loud boom sound."

"It happens all the time around here," Megan said. "After a while, you stop noticing it."

"I guess it's kind of like when Grant whines. At first it bothers me, but then I tune it out," Christina said and winked at her little brother.

"Huh?" Grant totally missed the analogy. "Is there an Air Force base around here?" he asked.

"There is, but that's not where these aircraft are coming from," Drew said. "Area 51 conducts regular testing and training missions of top-secret aircraft around Rachel.

Groom Lake, which is at the center of Area 51, is where they land them."

"They land them in water?" asked Grant.

"Oh, no. Groom Lake is a dry lake. So, they use it as a runway," Drew explained. "From the air, Groom Lake looks like a big abandoned salt mine."

"Not that you can ever fly over Area 51 to see it!" warned Megan. "It's in restricted air space!"

"I was talking about in maps," Drew clarified.

"The locals are the first to see many prototypes flying over Rachel," Megan said, changing the subject.

"A proto-what? Is that a jet?" Grant asked.

"A prototype is a model of something," explained Mimi. "The Air Force tests prototype aircraft out here in the desert. If they pass, they build more of them."

"Cool! If they're being tested, do they ever crash?" Grant asked.

"Yeah," Drew said. "A few years back two jets collided mid-air. One made it back; the other crashed right in the playground here in Rachel. No one was hurt, not even the pilot."

BOOM!

With Mimi in tow, Grant, Drew, and Megan raced outside to see the impromptu air show.

Christina stayed behind to replace a fallen alien bobble head. A woman wearing a Little A'Le'Inn T-shirt approached her.

"Christina? That *is* your name, right?" the woman asked, smacking her pink bubble gum.

Christina nodded.

"I'm not supposed to let customers use the phone," she said, popping a bubble, "but I'm going to make this one exception." She wagged her finger at Christina. "But next time, tell your boyfriend to call you on your cell phone, will ya?" The lady stood there with her hand outstretched, tapping her foot. "I'll take that!"

Christina exchanged the alien bobble head for the phone. "Don't be too long!" the woman ordered, shuffling away and muttering something about burgers burning.

Boyfriend? This must be some kind of mix-up, Christina thought. She lifted the receiver to her ear.

"Hello? This is Christina. Hello?" Silence! She was about to hang up when a robot-like voice on the other end said,

"HC61BOX8OALIEN! WHAT YOU SEEK IS HIDDEN IN PLAIN SIGHT!"

The line went dead.

Christina dashed over to the shelves lined with souvenirs to find a pen. She grabbed a glittery blue one with an alien head for a top. She decapitated the alien and jotted down the message on the palm of her hand. She breathed a sigh of relief and slid to the floor! Then, it hit her. *Whoever is leaving these clues has to be somewhere close by! And whoever it is knows my name!*

15
MUDDY BOOTS

Grant's voice seemed so distant. "Christeeeena! You in there?" Grant knocked on Christina's head.

"Don't knock on my head, Grant! Use water, use anything. But don't knock!" she warned.

"Sorry, Christina, but we're leaving now," Grant said as he helped her up.

Christina returned the pen to the shelf, but left the phone on the floor. She was too afraid Robot Voice would call her back!

They walked outside into the bright Nevada sunshine. "Why were you on the floor, anyway?" Grant asked.

"I'll tell you in the RV," Christina said.

"No can do! The RV is now a BDV!" Grant reported.

"A BDV?" Christina asked, confused.

"A Broken Down Vehicle!" Grant said, laughing at his own joke. "Anyway, we're going on a tour instead! There's Mimi. Come on!"

They met Mimi and their friends at what Grant called the "tour bus." Really, it was an old, small school bus painted to look like a UFO.

"This is Mr. Ellis," Mimi said. "He'll be your tour guide. I'll stay here with Papa. Hopefully, we can get a room here at the motel. If not, we still have our four-wheelers. It's not *that* far to the next town!" she joked.

The kids followed Mr. Ellis to the bus. "I'll get that," he said. He pulled hard on the bi-fold doors until they squeaked open.

The kids boarded the bus. A man wearing jeans and a cowboy hat low on his face sat in the back with his legs crossed at the ankles. Dried mud and grass caked the bottom of his boots. He was weaving a pen through his fingers.

The kids settled into their seats and waved good-bye to Mimi and Papa through the open window. A tow truck pulled out onto the highway hauling the RV behind it.

The man in the back of the bus chuckled loudly to himself. His boots scraped the floor when he stood up. He glared at the kids as he limped past. Christina noticed that his face was marked with fresh scrapes.

That's the guy from the mine shaft–the one who was driving the truck! Christina thought.

The kids waited until the man was off the bus before scrambling to the back.

"Hey, what's this?" Grant asked, picking up a small notepad from the seat. "Muddy Boots must have left it!" He examined it closely. "It's a flipbook!"

Starting from the back, Grant flipped through the pages. It was a mini-movie of two girls and two boys running through a field. A UFO appears out of one corner, moves across the page, and snatches them up in a beam of light. In the last frame, the UFO disappears too, and in its place stands a cow!

16
THE BLACK MAILBOX

They ducked down to the floor of the bus. "Did you recognize him, Grant?" Christina asked.

"Yeah, I recognized him! He was one of the guys in the mine! The bats got his face pretty good, huh?" Grant said. "And that limp! He must have hurt his leg running away from them!"

"That flipbook was meant to scare us!" Christina noted.

"Either that, or he's getting us back for the bat attack!" Grant exclaimed.

When the bus roared to life, the kids climbed back into their seats and buckled up.

"So, where to?" Mr. Ellis called over his shoulder.

"The Black Mailbox," Drew called out.

Muddy Boots watched the bus intently. As it drove by, he pointed two fingers at his eyes and then pointed to the kids as if to say, "I'm watching you!"

Christina shuddered.

"What's the Black Mailbox?" Grant asked.

"The famous Black Mailbox is just a mailbox," Drew said. "It's not black anymore, though. I heard the owner painted it white and bullet-proofed it!"

"Bullet-proofed it?" Grant asked.

"I heard it got shot at a lot," Drew explained.

Megan added, "It belongs to a guy who lives on E.T. Highway. Lots of tourists think it's the mailbox for Area 51, but it's not."

"Why's that?" Christina asked.

Megan continued, "It's right in front of a dirt road that leads to the main gate of Area 51."

"Why did you just call it E.T. Highway?" Grant asked.

"That's just what everyone calls it," she explained. She asked Mr. Ellis if he knew why.

"Back in the late 90s," their guide shouted over the rumbling bus engine, "they filmed the movie *Independence Day* around here. On the day the film was released in theaters, Highway 375 was officially given the name Extraterrestrial Highway."

"But, why E.T. Highway? Why not Independence Highway, after the film?" Grant shouted.

"The highway wasn't given its name because of any movie," Mr. Ellis said, looking at the kids in the rearview mirror. "It's called E.T. Highway because of all the UFO sightings near Area 51 and along this highway. All these people aren't here just for the alien burgers!"

"But if UFO sightings are so common around here, why don't we hear more about them?" Christina asked.

"I don't really know the answer to that," Mr. Ellis said. "Maybe some of the sightings out here are just experimental aircraft being tested. And others, well..."

"You'd think at least one would be a real UFO," Grant said. "It would be so cool to meet a real alien. Well, a nice one, anyway," he added.

"There's a group of scientists at the SETI Institute who believe aliens *must* exist. They devote their entire lives to the study of extraterrestrial life," Mr. Ellis explained.

"Oh, my aunt has a settee in her house," Grant said.

"No, S-E-T-I," Mr. Ellis said and laughed. "It stands for the 'Search for Extraterrestrial Intelligence.' The scientists at SETI believe their best hope of finding other forms of life in the universe is by communicating with them—or at least trying to communicate with them."

"Doesn't that mean that other life forms must be technologically advanced like us?" Christina asked.

"Maybe even more so," Mr. Ellis said.

"What if there is other life out there, but they can't communicate at all—like in the Stone Age?" Grant said.

"That's something to think about, isn't it?" Mr. Ellis said.

The kids nodded. Then, Grant turned to his sister and asked, "So, what happened back at the restaurant, anyway?"

"It was actually kind of creepy!" Christina replied. "Someone called me on the restaurant phone! The voice sounded robotic. And look at this!" She opened her palm to reveal the latest clue.

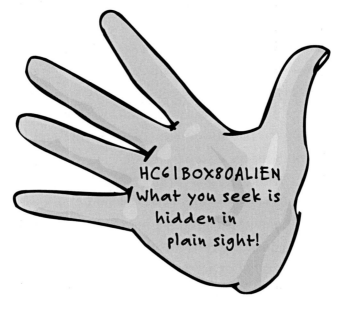

HC61BOX80ALIEN
what you seek is
hidden in
plain sight!

"There's HC again," Megan said. "Probably another address!"

The bus squeaked to a stop. "The Black Mailbox!" Mr. Ellis announced.

The kids ran to the mailbox. It was just that—a mailbox painted white. A cool breeze kicked up dust as traffic whizzed by. Craggy mountains dotted the horizon.

"The only thing missing is the chirping sound of crickets," Grant said, unimpressed. "Wait! Let me see your hand again, Christina! The clue is this mailbox! It even has the word ALIEN under the address!"

"But what about the warning, 'What you seek is hidden in plain sight!'?" Christina asked.

"I guess they're talking about the mailbox! It's hidden in plain sight, right?" Grant said.

"But, why *this* mailbox?" Christina asked.

Just then, Mr. Ellis handed the kids a rough map of the area. "I meant to give this to you earlier. We're right here." He pointed to the tiny mailbox icon.

"Thanks!" Grant said. Mr. Ellis walked off to answer a call on his cell phone.

Grant placed the map on top of the mailbox and flattened out the creases.

"The main gate to Area 51 is down that dirt road over there," Drew said, pointing.

"It's about 20 miles, according to this map," Megan noted.

I have to sit down, Christina thought. She was exhausted. She spied a boulder to plop down on. From where she sat, she could see the word ALIEN stenciled in black on the side of the mailbox. Then she noticed a small piece of paper clinging to the bottom of it.

"Grant," Christina yelled. "Under the mailbox!"

"I see it!" Grant said and reached for the paper. He accidentally dislodged it, causing it to blow away.

"Catch it!" Christina yelled.

Grant tackled the paper as it danced along the ground. Dust puffed around him as he landed in a heap. His arm flew up, waving the paper in the air like a truce flag.

It was another clue! Drew grabbed it and read,

373539.00N II55355.00W

Wait for the twinkling blanket to rise! The circle hides secrets that even the eyes up high don't see!

17
A TWINKLING BLANKET

"The numbers look like coordinates on a map," Christina said as she studied the mailbox clue.

"The N and W must mean *north* and *west*," noted Megan.

"But they're missing those little symbols," Christina said. She ran to borrow a pen from Mr. Ellis.

"Papa explained this to me once," Christina said. "There are three marks, and each represents a different distance. Each degree (she wrote o) is something like 70 miles on earth. The minutes (she wrote ′) are equal to a little over a mile each, and the seconds (she wrote ″) are some distance in feet," she explained.

She showed them the coordinates.

$$37°35'39.00''N\ 115°53'55.00''W$$

Christina punched the numbers into her cell phone. "Huh? The back gate of Area 51? There's a back gate, too?" she asked, perplexed.

"The back gate!" Grant repeated. "Look here, on Mr. Ellis's map! The road to the back gate starts here."

"It's not far from the Little A'Le'Inn!" Christina exclaimed. She clicked on the first entry. Images of the back gate of Area 51 popped up on the small screen. "It just looks like a regular toll booth on a highway," she said, unimpressed.

"Whoa! Check out the surveillance cameras, though!" Grant exclaimed. "Scroll down. Area 51 is crawling with guards!"

"Those are camo dudes!" Drew announced.

"Camo dudes?" Christina asked.

"They're guards dressed in camouflage. They protect the site 24-7," explained Drew.

"Site 24-7?" Grant asked. "Is that part of Area 51?"

"It's not a place, Grant," said Christina. "24-7 means twenty-four hours a day, seven days a week. What are they protecting *anyway*? The planes?"

"Nobody really knows! In fact, the government doesn't really admit that Area 51 exists!" Megan said.

Goosebumps rose on Christina's arms. *Why would someone lead us to a place the government won't even admit exists?* she wondered.

"Some people," Drew explained, "believe that UFOs and alien bodies recovered from crash sites are secretly studied at Area 51. They say some of the technology we use every day comes from what they've learned from the alien spacecraft!"

"I've even heard rumors that they have invisible runways!" Megan whispered. "Of course, it's all top secret and has never been proven. And the guards protecting Area 51 are authorized to use deadly force to keep it that way!"

They were interrupted by Mr. Ellis. "Kids, we need to start heading back. I promised I'd have you back by four," he shouted from the bus.

Megan read the clue again once the bus rumbled to life. "Wait for the twinkling blanket to rise! The circle hides secrets that even the eyes up high don't see!"

"I guess we have to go at night," Grant said. "A 'twinkling blanket' can mean only one thing, right? Unless, of course, Alien Baby has a twinkling pacifier *and* a twinkling blanket! Now, *that* would be really cool, huh?" he added.

"Grant, let's be serious," Christina said. Grant grinned and shrugged his shoulders.

"Well, it would be cool," he insisted.

"Anyway, let's go with the night theory," Christina said. "You mentioned seeing surveillance cameras in the photo, Grant. Maybe 'the eyes up high' refer to those cameras."

"What does the circle hide?" Megan asked.

"Wise man once say," Grant began, holding up a finger for effect, "discover what

circle *is*, then discover what circle *hides!*"
They all giggled.

Grant got serious. "If the clue is telling us to go at night, how do we convince Mimi and Papa to let us go?"

The kids grew quiet. They watched the Nevada desert fly by through the dirty bus windows.

Mr. Ellis parked his bus. "Thanks for the pen and for the tour!" Christina said, returning it to Mr. Ellis. The kids bounded out of the bus and ran out to greet Mimi and Papa in the parking lot.

Grant nudged Christina. "Look," he whispered.

On the side of the bus, painted in block letters was a sign: NIGHT TOURS.

"Excuse me, Mr. Ellis," Christina said. "About those night tours..."

18
A BULL BATTLE!

The kids ate an early dinner at the Little A'Le'Inn while Papa attached the trailer with the four-wheelers to the back of the tour bus.

"Two hours tops!" Papa reminded them.

"When we get to the entrance," Mr. Ellis announced, "I'll drive the bus the first five miles. Then, for the last three, we'll take the four-wheelers," he promised.

The sun was just setting in the west. A wash of pinks and purples hung on the horizon.

At the five-mile marker, Mr. Ellis pulled off the road and unloaded the four-wheelers. "Be careful! A lot can happen between here and the back gate. Look out for free-roaming cattle, and under NO circumstance should you go within twenty feet of the back gate! Those camo dudes mean business!"

"Look! The desert's on fire!" Grant exclaimed.

Mr. Ellis chuckled. "No, son, those are alien enthusiasts trying to keep warm. I mentioned on the bus that people from all over the world come to this town. Well, this is where they come! They're scanning the skies for alien spaceships! Now, just follow the road ahead of you," he shouted over the rumbling engines.

Christina gave the thumbs up and took off down the road with the others in tow.

"WHOOOOOOA!" Suddenly, a snorting, coal-black bull appeared in front of Christina. She slammed on her brakes and careened off to the side of the road.

Luckily, Drew, Megan, and Mr. Ellis were far enough back to stop safely. Grant wasn't so lucky. He screeched to a halt right in front of the bull. It snorted loudly and backed up a few steps, flicking its tail. Grant revved his engine. The bull snorted again and lumbered off in the opposite direction.

Grant removed his helmet, panting from the close encounter. "Grant, put it back on!" Christina screamed. "It's getting ready to charge!"

Grant looked up. The bull was facing him again! Its head was low. It scraped its hoof on the ground. Grant frantically popped his helmet on his head just as the bull charged. Grant veered off the road and drove as fast as his four-wheeler would safely go. The bull chased him a good ways into the desert before giving up and trotting off, snorting and shaking its head.

The kids followed Grant into an open field where a giant circle of shoulder-high grass rose in front of them.

Christina jumped off her four-wheeler and ran to Grant. His helmet was off, and he was leaning over the handlebars of his vehicle. "Grant," Christina said, "are you—"

"That...was...awesome!" Grant yelled. He threw his helmet up into the air. It landed in the sea of tall grass.

"Grant! You're OK!" Christina said, relieved.

"That was a close one!" Drew shouted.

The kids looked back. "Mr. Ellis?" Megan called. "I thought he was behind us."

"We better head back to the road," Christina advised.

"My helmet!" Grant exclaimed.

"We'll have to go in for it," Christina said, looking at the tall grass.

"Anyone want to draw straws again?" Grant teased. "JK!"

They marched into the grass and searched for the helmet. "We'll need our flashlights!" Grant decided. "It's too dark out here!"

"They're on the four-wheelers," Megan said.

"Wait!" Christina whispered. "Do you hear that?"

WHIRRRR! WHIRRRR! A whirling sound got closer and closer and louder and louder. "Duck!" Christina yelled. They lay there hidden in the tall grass, hearts pounding.

Hovering above them was that disc-shaped UFO again! Blinding white lights swirled around it as it hummed hypnotically.

It glided to the right, then to the left. *It must be searching for us!* Christina thought.

The object skimmed the top of the grass a few feet from where they crouched, then suddenly whizzed away.

Grant stood up. "What are you doing, Grant?" Christina cried, trying to grab him. "It might come back and suck us up like in that flipbook!"

"It's gone, Christina," Grant assured her.

"It's safe to get the flashlights! Let's go, Megan!" Christina said. The girls raced to retrieve their flashlights from the four-wheelers and sprinted back.

"What was that last clue again?" Grant asked.

"The circle hides secrets that even the eyes up high don't see," Drew said from memory, still shaking from the close encounter. "This giant grass circle fits with the clue, right?" he said.

"Hey, did someone drop their flashlight?" Megan asked, pointing at something shining in the grass. Grant leaned down to get a better look at it.

"No, it's some type of handle!" Grant exclaimed and turned it. A secret door popped open. "It's a tunnel!"

"What's a tunnel doing out here in the middle of a crop field?" Megan asked.

"I don't know!" Christina exclaimed. "But this must be what the circle is hiding!"

19

A PICTURE'S WORTH A THOUSAND WORDS

"We've got to go down there!" Christina said.

"But Mr. Ellis must be looking for us!" Drew said. "Megan and I will ride back and say that we got split up. We'll wait for you at the road."

Grant and Christina watched their friends leave.

"Ready?" Christina asked, pointing to the tunnel.

"Ready!" Grant said.

They climbed down the metal ladder and shut the access door. Christina wedged a rock in the opening to keep from getting locked in.

"It's a secret room!" Grant exclaimed. He found a camping lantern and switched it on.

"Look, we've hit the jackpot!" Christina squealed. She was standing next to a table stacked with aerial maps of local ranches. Christina leafed through them. "Here's a map of the Flyin' R! That's Buck's ranch!"

"And, look, someone has marked the back entrance of the property with a red X!" Grant exclaimed. "What's this?" he asked, pointing to a chart.

"It looks like a schedule," Christina said. She ran her finger across the top of the chart and stopped at FR. "The Flyin' R!" she exclaimed. From FR, she ran her finger down and stopped at an icon. Tomorrow's date was written in pen inside a little UFO.

"Something's going to happen at the ranch tomorrow!" she exclaimed.

A file slid off the table and slapped the floor. The contents spilled out. Grant leaned down to pick it up.

"Christina, it's us!" he shouted, holding up a stack of black and white photos.

"Someone's been tailing us!" He flipped through the pile. "And look at these!"

Grant's hand shook as he held up shots of gray, pasty-looking aliens silhouetted by a bright light. They were standing on a ramp. One of the aliens faced the camera. Its bug eyes reminded Christina of the creepy UFO book back at the ranch house! She shuddered.

Christina pulled out her cell phone and began snapping photos. The maps. SNAP! The schedule. SNAP! The photos. SNAP!

"Grant, what's that?" Christina asked.

In a corner of the room, a white sheet covered something lying on the floor. Grant leaned down and pulled the edge up. "It's an alien!" he screamed and dropped the sheet. Still uncovered was its long, slender hand. Its fingertips were bony and had no fingernails!

"Let's get out of here!" Grant screamed and dropped the lantern. He scrambled up the ladder.

Christina took a deep breath and tiptoed over to the sheet. "I can't believe I am going to do this," she mumbled, and pulled it back slowly. Alien. SNAP! She dropped the sheet and scooted up the ladder.

Christina peeked inside the hideout once more. The lantern lit up the room. "Grant!" Christina squealed. "There are three more of them!"

Christina was about to close the hatch when Grant stopped her.

"The lamp! I dropped it!" Grant yelled. "They'll know we got in!"

"I left my flashlight, too! But, do we really want to go back down there?" she asked, still shaking.

"No way! Those things might just be sleeping! And they don't look that friendly!" Grant squealed. Christina snapped one last photo of the hideout entrance before slamming the hatch shut.

As he started to leave, Grant noticed something shiny in the grass. "My helmet!" he cried. "But, but, how...?"

"Let's go!" Christina yelled.

20
SHADOW GUARD

Christina and Grant found their friends and their guide waiting for them by the paved road.

"Sorry, kids," Mr. Ellis said. "My four-wheeler stalled after that bull encounter! I've heard stories of bulls charging people around here, but I've never seen one do that in the flesh! This place is usually **teeming** with cattle, too! That was some amazing off-road driving, kid!"

"I thought I was a goner for sure!" Grant exclaimed. "And on top of that, we found—"

Christina silenced her brother with a sharp jab to the ribs. "Ouch!" Grant yelled.

"The desert can be a real spooky place, huh?" Mr. Ellis said. "Well, we still have an hour left. We're not far from the back gate!"

"I think I've had enough fun for one night!" Grant said. The others nodded.

Just then, a dark pickup truck came barreling down the road. It veered off into the field. Seconds later, they watched as its headlights did a full circle and headed back in their direction!

"That's Muddy Boots' truck!" whispered Christina.

"On second thought," Grant said to Mr. Ellis, "as long as we're here, it would be a pity not to see the back gate."

"You won't have to ask *me* twice!" Christina squealed, jumping back on her four-wheeler.

They took off towards the back gate of Area 51. As the rumble of the truck's engine grew louder, Christina glanced back. Mr. Ellis had pulled over and was waving his flashlight above his head.

Muddy Boots blasted his horn as he zoomed past him.

The kids were fast approaching the back gate, which was lit up like a beacon in the night. NO TRESPASSING! WARNING! STOP! The signs loomed large ahead of them.

They skidded to a stop right in front of the gate. The kids jumped off their four-wheelers and scrambled down an embankment to escape Muddy Boots. Suddenly, blinding lights switched on! Coming towards them were four silhouetted figures with bright, shiny red eyes!

"Aliens!" shouted Grant. "They're going to suck our brains out!"

"AAAAAHHHHH!" they screamed.

The mysterious figures grabbed the kids by the arms and hauled them to the gate. The kids tried to wiggle free, but the grip was too strong!

"Wait! Sir, those kids are with me. I'm very sorry!" Mr. Ellis apologized, out of breath. "They got spooked and took off!"

The kids swung around and looked at their captors. "We can arrest you for trespassing!" warned the tallest guard who was built like a bodybuilder. "But since you have an adult with you, we'll let you go."

"Camo dudes! What a relief!" said Grant. "I thought the aliens had us for sure! But the red eyes? The bright lights?"

"Night vision goggles and big flashlights," Bodybuilder Guard explained.

"Hey, can we get a picture taken with you?" Grant asked excitedly.

"I could lose my job over it, kid," he said, looking away from them. "You have a safe ride back now."

Grant turned to his sister. She was staring beyond the gate into Area 51. She looked terrified! Then he saw it, too! A tall, slender figure was watching them from the shadows of the guardhouse. Its eyes glowed red. It moved out of the shadows and stepped towards them!

Grant and Christina took a step back. "Christina! He's just another camo dude! Look!" Grant whispered.

Shadow Guard approached the gate. He was wearing sunglasses even though it was night. "Is everything all right here?"

"Yeah, they were just leaving," another guard said, crossing his arms.

The kids headed back to their four-wheelers. Christina glanced back at the gate. Shadow Guard's eyes glowed red as he watched them leave!

21
A STORM AND A SCOWL

Their motel room at the Little A'Le'Inn was in a converted trailer with a shared bathroom and kitchen. From the "evidence room," as the lady behind the counter called it, they picked out a movie involving aliens called *Close Encounters of the Third Kind*. Five minutes into the film, Papa found them sprawled out on the floor fast asleep.

In the morning, they sat down to a warm, inviting breakfast of scrambled eggs, toast, and jelly. They washed it down with piping hot cocoa.

"We need to be on the road in twenty!" Papa announced.

"What about the RV?" Grant asked.

"It arrived at sunrise! The mechanic's last words after waking me from my slumber were, 'Sir, I suggest you turn that one in for a new one!'" Papa roared with laughter and slapped the table.

"What? The RV's not fixed?" asked Christina.

"He assured me it was, but I'm not taking any chances. Besides, a storm's approaching," Papa warned. He checked his watch. "And the twenty minutes start now!"

Mimi and Papa chuckled as they watched the kids sprint out the door to collect their things from the motel room.

The wind was already picking up. The sky was a dark, half-open dome of clouds that was rapidly closing over them. They shoved everything into duffel bags and dashed out to the RV.

"My cell phone!" Christina exclaimed. "I must have left it in the room!" She found it resting on the TV and sprinted back out the door to meet the others.

A man with a cowboy hat pulled down low over his scowling face waited behind the motel trailer. His muddy boots kicked up dust as he limped away empty-handed!

22
A DIRTY CLUE!

The RV rumbled down the highway. Lightning flashed and rain pelted the windows. Christina downloaded the pictures of the hidden lair onto her laptop.

"See here," Grant said, pointing to the computer screen. "These are pictures of us! Someone's been tailing us!"

Megan and Drew moved in closer, shocked by what they saw on the screen.

"And this is a schedule," Christina said. "Apparently, someone is planning to trespass onto the Flyin' R sometime today."

"Won't they change their plans, Christina? They know we were down there in their hideout," Grant said.

"I doubt they know we're linked to any of the ranches. To them, we're just a bunch of nosy kids on vacation," Christina said hopefully.

"Unless—" Grant said. "Take a look at this photo."

In the last photo Christina had taken outside of the hideout, the entrance was blurry, but the background was in perfect focus. They saw a man crouched a few feet from the hideout opening. His image was cut off from the neck up, so they couldn't see his face. His clothes were those of a typical ranch hand, except for a gem-studded bolo tie around his neck!

"That's Ol' Zeb in the photo!" Megan cried.

"I recognized the bolo tie, too," Christina confessed.

"But what's he doing out there?" she asked.

No one said anything.

"Grant said someone was tailing us and taking pictures," Megan said. She looked ready to cry.

"We don't know if he's involved, Megan," Christina said.

Megan didn't look convinced. "Christina, he's crouched down in the grass, just feet from a secret hole in the ground full of alien bodies, maps, and schedules! That makes him look pretty guilty!"

Megan had a point. Christina crossed her arms and looked out the window. The sky was a swirling mass of dark clouds. BOOM! CRACK! The sky exploded like fireworks!

"Christina, I need to call Nina to warn her!" Megan cried.

"Warn her of what?" Christina asked. "Megan, he was there at the hideout. He could have locked us in there, but he didn't."

Megan thought about Christina's logic but was still unconvinced. She shook her head and stared out the window.

Christina wasn't convinced either. *He might have just arrived at the hideout and we caught him by surprise,* Christina thought, but she kept that to herself.

"Check this out!" Grant squealed. On the computer screen was a picture of a clue scrawled in the dirt in front of their motel!

Christina gasped. "So, someone broke into our motel room to use *my* camera phone to take a picture of a clue?!"

"Looks that way! I mean, these are the pictures from your phone, right?" said Grant.

"They must have gone in while we were eating breakfast!" Christina said. She shuddered.

"What does the clue say?" Megan asked

8.30
The UFOs don't lie!
Go back to the red X!

"X?" Grant exclaimed. "This morning, I saw a big X in the dirt in front of our motel room. I didn't give it much thought, though. You know, nothing gets between me and my breakfast!"

"Maybe whoever wrote this realized that we missed that clue," Christina guessed. "They had to make sure we saw it, so they used my phone!"

"But breaking into a motel room? That seems kind of drastic—and risky!" Megan said.

"This clue must be really important, then," Christina said. She pulled up the aerial map of the Flyin' R and pointed to the red X at the back of the property. "This has to be the meeting spot," she said.

"What about the UFO icons?" Grant asked. "Is the Flyin' R going to be attacked by aliens?"

"I don't know," Christina said.

"The numbers have to be the time, then!" Megan exclaimed.

"So, 8:30 tonight," Grant whispered. He could barely get the words out.

23
THE MOTHER SHIP

Leaves and branches littered the driveway. Dark, billowing clouds hung low in the sky, threatening a repeat of the storm that had just swept the ranch.

The RV took its last breath as Papa pulled up to Buck's ranch house. "The Flyin' R!" Papa roared. Everyone spilled out of the RV, happy to be back.

After dinner, the kids were given the go-ahead to do some night riding on their four-wheelers. "I want you back at the first sign of lightning *and* steer clear of the lake! I'm not too fond of night fishing," Buck said, chuckling.

With Megan in the lead, the kids navigated the muddy path to the back of the ranch. Christina pulled alongside Megan and motioned for them to stop.

"What's that?" she asked.

"That's Ol' Zeb's trailer," Drew said.

"Where's the back gate from here?" Christina asked.

"See those trees?" Megan asked. "They encircle a big field where the cattle like to graze. The back gate is at the far side of that field."

Christina checked the time on her cell phone. "We're early," she said.

"Ol' Zeb's truck is gone and the lights in his trailer are off," Drew remarked.

"We can hide there, on his porch. It's dry, at least," Christina suggested.

"Aren't you afraid this might be a trap? He could be a brain-sucking alien!" Grant declared.

"If he were a brain-sucking alien, Grant, he could have finished us off a long time ago," Christina said.

"Guess that's true," answered Grant with a shrug.

They dismounted their four-wheelers and headed to the trailer. "Where's Grant?" Christina whispered. "Hey, what's that springy noise?"

"Here I am!" Grant yelled.

SQUISH! BOING! SQUISH! BOING! "Look, I found a pogo stick!" Grant shouted.

"Quit fooling around!" she warned. "Grant, watch out!"

PLUNK! Grant crash-landed on Ol' Zeb's porch. A flower pot shattered and scattered dirt across the wooden planks. He popped up. "I'm OK!"

"Grant, we have to keep the noise down!" Christina warned.

"OK, sorry!" Grant exclaimed.

"A key!" Megan announced. "I think it was under the flower pot!" Carefully, she unlocked the door.

The door creaked open. They slid inside and shut the door behind them. "A lantern!" Grant announced.

"No, no lantern! We can't give away our hiding place. No matter what!" Christina hissed.

"Is it just me, or is no one else worried about how this might turn out?" Megan asked. She looked worried.

"Whoever left us this last clue went to a lot of trouble to get it to us, right?" Christina began. "For some reason, they trust us to help solve this mystery!"

Just then, they heard a crackling noise, and then a squeaky voice. "The mother ship is ready for landing."

"It's a radio!" Grant exclaimed. They crawled over to the panel of blinking lights.

"Target in view. I repeat, target in view," the squeaky voice repeated.

"The aliens are coming!" Grant cried.

"Come on, let's get to the back gate!" Christina urged.

"They won't see us if we follow the tree line," Megan suggested.

They opened the door of the trailer and slipped out. Blanketed by the night, they crept along through the trees, careful not to make even the slightest sound.

Megan pulled at Christina's jacket and pointed at something in the distance. Coming in low were six bright lights.

"The mother ship!" Grant exclaimed.

"They're flying awfully low," Megan noted.

"Come on, we're still too far away!" Christina urged.

The kids raced through the trees. Suddenly, Christina stopped, holding out her arms to block the others from going any further.

"There's a break in the tree line! I didn't expect this," Christina said, leaning over, trying to catch her breath. "Grant, are you still wearing your helmet?"

"Yeah! It'll make it harder for them to suck my brains out!" he reasoned.

"Umm, yeah," she said, trying not to laugh. "On the count of three, OK?" Christina whispered.

"Stay low to the ground, so they can't see us!" Drew warned.

They took off running. Out of nowhere, the disc-shaped UFO they had seen before flew past them, then doubled back.

"Not again!" Christina whimpered.

It was too late! They had been spotted! The UFO hovered just above them, then dove!

"Run!" Christina yelled. They all darted in different directions, making the UFO spin out of control. CRASH! It flew into a tree!

The kids tumbled to the ground and covered their heads, waiting for an explosion. Nothing! They crawled over to the creaking heap. Smoke billowed out of the top.

"Grant, get down from there!" Christina warned.

"I just want to see the aliens! They're probably knocked out!" Grant whispered. He unlatched the top. Wires spilled out. "Huh? No aliens?"

The other kids climbed up onto the massive heap of metal and peered inside.

"It looks like some kind of video camera!" Drew said.

"That means someone knows we're here now!" Megan cried.

"We can't worry about that right now!" Christina insisted. "Look, the mother ship has landed! See, the lights aren't moving anymore."

They slid down the metal heap and raced through the tree line towards the back gate. The kids hunkered down behind a mountain of hay bales.

"What are you doing, Grant?" Christina asked.

"Camouflage!" Grant said, stuffing hay into his shirt.

"Really?" Christina asked, exasperated.

From their perch, the kids saw the mother ship. It was hard to make out because the light pouring from it was blinding. They watched in awe as three ramps opened up like a giant yawning before bedtime. More dazzling lights poured out.

"Look!" Grant gasped. He was shaking hay from helmet to toe. "Aliens!"

"Oh, man! I should have worn my helmet, too!" Drew cried. "Grant, give me some of your hay!"

"No way! Get your own!" Grant replied.

Three silhouetted forms with long arms and protruding chests suddenly appeared. When they turned, light filtered through their bulging eyes. The figures disappeared down the ramp.

A fourth alien appeared at the base of the mother ship. He seemed to communicate with the others using a series of clicks and whistles.

"They're stealing our cattle!" Megan said angrily.

One by one, cows were herded into the mouth of the mother ship. Suddenly, one of the cows turned back. The fourth alien limped up the ramp as he redirected the stray back into ship.

"That's no alien—he's limping!" Christina whispered to the others.

"That's Muddy Boots!" Grant exclaimed.

"And that's no mother ship!" Megan said. Those are cattle transport trucks sitting side by side!"

"I get it now!" Christina yelped. "Muddy Boots and his crew are modern-day cattle rustlers posing as alien cow abductors!"

Muddy Boots flipped a switch at the base of the truck. The first ramp closed, shutting Buck's cattle inside.

Christina sensed that someone was watching them. She turned and saw Ol' Zeb hidden in a grove of trees. He seemed to float out of the trees and move in their direction.

"Ol' Zeb," Christina whispered to the others. The others turned to look. Ol' Zeb placed a finger over his lips. He pointed to his chest and then to the truck.

They watched as the spry old man sprinted with ease toward the trucks. He bounded up the open ramp and disappeared inside.

Just then, a series of clicks and whistles came from inside the trailer. They grew louder and louder. The four "aliens" turned to listen. "What was that?" one of them asked.

"That guy just blew his cover!" Grant whispered and rolled his eyes.

Muddy Boots motioned to his buddies to follow him up the ramp to investigate.

"Megan, do you know how to herd cattle?" Christina asked.

"Buck taught me a thing or two! Wanna learn?" she asked with a mischievous grin.

With swift movements and hushed commands, the children expertly directed the corralled cattle up the ramp and into the truck. There was no hope of escape for Muddy Boots and his fake alien crew.

Grant and Drew sprinted to the back of the truck and flipped the switch. They watched as the ramp closed shut, trapping the cattle rustlers inside!

24
A BOLO TIE IN DISGUISE!

As stars littered the night sky, the cattle rustlers were taken into custody by the local sheriff. Their realistic alien disguises hung in tatters from their bodies, compliments of the cattle they tried to steal!

Those aliens in the hideout must have been costumes! thought Christina.

"Kids, that was some fine detective work!" the sheriff said. "We've been trying to solve this cattle alien abduction mystery for three years now! It looks like those alien posers were taking advantage of the mystery surrounding Area 51 to cover up their cattle rustling operation!" he exclaimed. He continued to brag on the kids to his deputy as he walked to his patrol car.

Muddy Boots and his crew sat squished in the back of the patrol car. As the sheriff sped off with lights swirling and sirens blaring, Muddy Boots craned his neck to glare at the kids through the back window.

After learning of their adventures, Mimi and Papa were relieved that the kids were safe. "You can imagine our surprise when you called, Christina. At worst, we thought one of you had run out of gas!" Mimi said.

"Instead, we learned that you children managed to solve one of the longest-running mysteries around these parts!" Papa said, tousling Grant's hay-sprinkled hair.

"At least we steered clear of the lake, Buck!" Drew said, grinning from ear to ear.

"That's a good thing indeed!" Buck agreed. He threw his head back and laughed heartily.

"We'll go back to the house with Buck and Nina. Will you kids be all right getting back on the four-wheelers?" Mimi asked. Then she thought about all the adventures they'd been through. "Silly question, huh?"

"Even kid detectives need someone to worry about them," Christina said, smiling.

Once the rear lights of the truck bounced away, the kids mounted their four-wheelers, popped on their helmets, and started back to the house.

The kids passed by the UFO crash site. The giant heap of metal no longer creaked and groaned! Smoke had long since stopped seeping from its top.

It's hard to believe we were so afraid of that thing! Christina thought. *It won't bother us anymore!*

"Megan?" Christina looked around. Megan had stopped her four-wheeler in front of the crash site. Her figure was outlined by the night sky. They doubled back for her.

"Where did Ol' Zeb go? He was there and then he wasn't!" Megan whispered, looking back in the direction of the cattle trucks. The blue lights of the patrol cars lit up the scene as the deputies collected evidence. The UFO would soon be hauled away, too.

"Ol' Zeb probably went back home," Christina guessed.

"But we saw him run into the truck trailer. How did he get out without our seeing him?" Drew asked.

"Let's go find out!" Christina shouted. "Follow me!"

Christina led them back to Ol' Zeb's trailer. They found the door wide open with warm lamp light spilling out onto the porch. The kids looked at each other wide-eyed and raced inside.

"Ol' Zeb?" Megan called.

"There's nothing here!" Grant shouted. The place was completely empty. It looked like no one had ever lived in the old trailer.

"We were just here!" Drew exclaimed. "And the radio equipment! It's gone, too!"

"He's really gone! I feel so bad about suspecting him of being one of the bad guys!" Megan said remorsefully.

"We all suspected him!" Drew said, trying to make his sister feel better.

"He must have been the one to leave all of the clues. It makes sense, right?" Christina said.

"But why didn't he solve the mystery by himself?" Grant asked. "He knew where all the hideouts were. He led us to them, right?"

"I think he needed us to help him along the way," Christina said. "By solving one clue, we uncovered more evidence for Ol' Zeb."

"We did a great job trapping those fake aliens, didn't we?" Grant said.

"You said it!" Drew agreed. They slapped high fives and took off outside. BOING! SQUISH! BOING! SQUISH! Christina and Megan smiled at each other. Grant was on the pogo stick again!

The girls turned to leave. *It would have been nice to hear his side of the story!* Christina thought, and then she laughed.

"Why are you laughing?" Megan asked.

"I was just thinking that Ol' Zeb must have been tailing us this whole time," Christina explained.

"So you *do* think he was the one taking those pictures?" Megan asked incredulously.

"No, that was Muddy Boots and his UFO video camera, I'm sure," Christina explained. "I think Ol' Zeb was protecting us, you know, like at the ranch with those snakes. I was laughing because he must have seen all the crazy stuff we did, like Grant being chased by the bull," Christina explained.

"We must have been a sight to see!" Megan agreed, laughing.

They walked out of the trailer and shut the door behind them. "The light! We forgot to turn it off," Christina said, and ran back inside.

"Everyone! Come in here!" Christina yelled.

They scrambled into the trailer.

"On the wall!" Christina gasped.

There, hanging from a rusted hook on an otherwise bare wall hung a gem-studded bolo tie!

Christina removed it from the hook and studied the stone. "It's like nothing I've ever seen before!" Even the color of the stone was indescribable. She held it up to the light to get a better look at it.

They watched as the gem lit up, then cast a brilliant beam of multicolored light onto the far wall!

"No way!" Grant squealed. "Another clue!"

The beam coming from Ol' Zeb's bolo tie projected a clue onto the wall:

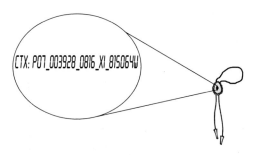

CTX: P07_003928_0816_XI_815064W

"Quick, Grant! Grab my phone. It's in my jacket pocket!" Christina commanded.

"It's not over?" Drew asked. He shook his head in disbelief.

Grant grabbed the phone and looked up the numbers on the Internet.

"What does it say?" Christina asked. The image on the wall began to blur.

"Inca City," Grant said.

"Inca City, as in Peru?" Christina said.

"No, not Peru, not anywhere near Peru. Not anywhere on this earth!" Grant said.

Christina joined the others gathered around the cell phone.

"It's Inca City on Mars!" Grant announced. "Those are coordinates on Mars! It says here that they named that spot Inca City because it looks like an ancient Incan city in Peru," Grant explained.

"Does this mean he wants us to go there?" Megan said. "Impossible!"

"You said it yourself! Area 51 is a mysterious place," Christina said. She handed the bolo tie to Megan. "Ol' Zeb would want you to have this. Maybe one day, we'll figure out what this clue means."

"Oh, I've already figured it out!" Grant proclaimed. "Ol' Zeb is like this cool member of the galactic police force, zooming through space and catching bad guys, no matter where they are!"

"Or, he could be just a ranch hand who happens to know a lot about planets and stuff!" Christina said.

"Well, I do know one thing!" Grant said.

"What's that?" Christina asked.

"I'm hungry! Let's go back to the house and rustle up some food. Get it? Rustle?" Grant said, grinning from ear to ear.

"Yeah, we get it," Christina said, shaking her head and laughing.

Just then, Grant shouted, "Look! A shooting star!"

Christina was quiet. She knew shooting stars only fell *towards* Earth, not away from it! The four kids quietly watched as the light grew smaller and smaller. It finally disappeared among the millions of stars sprinkling the night sky.

"Goodbye, Ol' Zeb," Christina whispered softly, "if that *is* you!"

Well, that was fun!

Wow, glad we solved that mystery!

Where shall we go next?

EVERYWHERE!

The End

Now...go to
www.carolemarshmysteries.com
and...

• Add this book to your personal Adventure Map Tracker!

• Go on a Scavenger Hunt!

• Take a Pop(corn) Quiz!

• Hear from Mimi, Papa, Christina, and Grant!

• Talk to Christina and Grant!

• Join the Fan Club...and MUCH MORE!

GLOSSARY

abandoned: deserted; left behind

abduction: being kidnapped

antics: behavior

authenticity: being genuine; real

authorized: given permission

collective: happening as a group

cringe: to fear; cower

disarray: disordered; not organized

evidence: a sign that proves something

rustler: one who steals cattle

SAT GLOSSARY

abdomen: the belly

ailment: a physical or mental disorder

homonym: words that sound the same and may be spelled the same, but have different meanings

outskirts: away from the center; the border

teeming: to be filled with, especially living things

Enjoy this exciting excerpt from:

THE MYSTERY AT
Cape Cod

1
WHAT'S A CAPE COD?

"Wake up," yelled Grant, shaking Christina's arm. "Papa says there's Cape Cod!"

Christina's blue eyes flew open just as Papa dipped the left wing of his little red and white airplane, the *Mystery Girl*. She peered out the window. Her stick-straight brown hair danced around her shoulders. She was excited! Below was the sparkling white coastline of Cape Cod, their vacation destination.

"I don't get it," said Grant, disappointment in his voice. "I don't see a cape, and I don't see a cod."

"Actually, Cape Cod is a peninsula," said Mimi, closing her guidebook.

"What's a pen-soo-la?" asked Grant.

"A peninsula," said Mimi, emphasizing the correct pronunciation of the word, "is a piece of land almost surrounded by water. Cape Cod juts out into the Atlantic Ocean. See?" As Mimi pointed out the window, a cluster of sparkly red bracelets jangled on her wrist.

Mimi read a few lines from her guidebook about how great glaciers formed Cape Cod thousands and thousands of years ago. "See those rolling hills down there near the coast line?" she asked. "They are called drumlins. They were shaped by the glaciers."

"Wow!" said Grant. "You mean ice moved across the land and pushed up all those rocks and sand down there into the ocean to make Cape Cod?"

"That's right," said Mimi.

"You know, your grandma spent a lot of time in Cape Cod when she was younger," said Papa, pushing back his black cowboy hat. He patted Mimi's hand. "That was before I knew her."

"Yes," said Mimi. "I had just graduated from college. Some girlfriends and I came to Cape Cod because we wanted to write. We joined a group of writers living in the town of Truro. We thought it sounded romantic."

"What was Cape Cod like back then?" asked Christina.

"A lot like it is now," said Mimi. "100-foot sand dunes. Windswept marshes. Wild, pink beach roses growing in between the rocks. Weathered houses, windmills, and lighthouses. Of course, the Cape is a lot more crowded now, especially Provincetown." Mimi sighed.

"Did you write a mystery book while you were there, Mimi?" asked Christina. She was proud that her grandma was Carole Marsh, the famous writer of children's mysteries. Papa flew the *Mystery Girl* all over the world so Mimi could do research for her novels. Christina and Grant traveled with their grandparents whenever they could.

"No, I just thought about it," replied Mimi, winking.

"What's all that red stuff down there?" asked Grant with his nose plastered against the plane's window. "It looks like a huge bowl of cherries."

"Those must be the cranberry bogs," said Papa. "It's more like a huge bowl of cranberries. Half of the cranberries harvested in the world are grown on Cape Cod."

"Can you tell that Cape Cod is shaped like a giant bent arm?" asked Mimi. "The town of Bourne is located at its shoulder. Chatham, where we are staying, is at the elbow. And Provincetown, where we are landing, is on the fist."

"It looks like a giant fishhook to me," Grant said. "That's it, it's a giant hook with a cod on it!" He giggled at his own joke. "Get it?"

Mimi and Papa smiled as Grant shoved his new iPod ear buds back into his ears. His eyes closed and his head of unruly blond hair swayed to the music.

"Did you know Cape Cod is where they transmitted the very first wireless message?" Papa said loudly, glancing over his shoulder at Grant.

"What?" shouted Grant.

"First wireless message. Cape Cod!" Papa shouted back.

Grant gave a "thumbs up" and kept jiving. Papa's wireless message was definitely not getting through!

Christina rolled her eyes at her brother. "Are we going to Truro, Mimi?"

"Yes, Sweetie, I think we will stay with my old friend's daughter Arabella and her husband Ben at their cottage in Chatham for two nights. Then we'll go to Truro for a day. We'll have a nice, relaxing vacation—no researching. No mysteries for us!"

"You always say that," said Christina, teasing her blond, blue-eyed grandma, who was pulling her cherry red sweater up around her shoulders. Mimi smiled at Christina, her eyes twinkling.

Suddenly, Papa's radio blared.

"*Mystery Girl*, this is Provincetown Air Traffic Control. Weather conditions indicate that a nor'easter is developing off the coast of Maine. Its projected path includes the entire New England coast. Landfall may occur within 48 to 72 hours. This storm could bring precipitation, gale force winds, rough seas, and coastal flooding. Please divert your landing from Provincetown to Boston's Logan Airport!"